Sensible Shoes

STUDY GUIDE

Sharon Garlough Brown
Sharron Carrns

IVP Books

An imprint of InterVarsity Press
Downers Grove, Illinois

InterVarsity Press
P.O. Box 1400, Downers Grove, IL 60515-1426
ivpress.com
email@ivpress.com

*InterVarsity Press® is the book-publishing division of InterVarsity Christian Fellowship/USA®, a
movement of students and faculty active on campus at hundreds of universities, colleges, and schools
of nursing in the United States of America, and a member movement of the International Fellowship
of Evangelical Students. For information about local and regional activities, visit intervarsity.org.*

Cover design: Cindy Kiple
Interior design: Daniel van Loon
*Images: group of women holding hands: JupiterImages/Getty Images
        small girl sitting on suitcase: susan.k./Getty Images*

ISBN 978-0-8308-4333-6 (print)
ISBN 978-0-8308-8901-3 (digital)

Printed in the United States of America ∞

P 25 24 23 22 21 20 19 18 17 16 15 14 13 12 11 10 9 8

Y 36 35 34 33 32 31 30 29 28 27 26 25 24 23 22 21

Contents

Introduction

The most common thing I hear from readers of *Sensible Shoes* is "I saw bits of myself in each character but especially in [fill in the blank]." I'm also frequently asked, "What next steps can I take in my journey with God? I want to take a sacred journey like the characters!"

This study guide is designed with these reader responses in mind. You are invited to travel in a directed way for three months, just like the characters do at the New Hope Center. This guide provides twelve weeks of daily Scripture reading, prayer, and reflection questions (five days a week). Given that it's often easier to see truth in others' lives before we see it in ourselves, you'll have questions to answer about how the characters are responding to (or resisting) the presence and love of God. Then you'll be invited to consider your own life with God. I hope the characters will become windows and mirrors into seeing yourself more clearly. I also hope you'll take seriously the invitation to travel with others. We aren't meant to walk alone. With that in mind, there are group discussion questions offered at the end of each week.

You can decide whether to read *Sensible Shoes* first in its entirety and then return to do a slow study with the guide, or to read it a section at a time, matching your pace to the daily questions. Commit to keeping a travelogue of your journey. Even if you aren't in the habit of using a journal, you'll benefit from keeping a record of what you're noticing as you move forward. Not every question will resonate with you. That's okay. You don't need to answer every question every day. But do watch for any impulse to avoid a question because it agitates you or makes you feel uncomfortable. That's probably the very question you need to spend some time pondering! If you don't have time to answer the questions you want to reflect on, simply mark them and return later.

Some questions and themes are repeated as you journey with the guide, and you may be tempted to say, "I already answered that." Listen with fresh ears. Is anything new emerging? Shifting? Coming into sharper focus? Use the questions as launching points for your journaling. If something in the chapter speaks to you and isn't addressed in a question, spend some time journaling and praying about it. One of the primary themes of the book is learning to pay attention to the things that stir us, both the positive and the negative. As the retreat leader, Katherine, says, "Stay with what stirs you."

One more suggestion: as you prepare each day, offer a prayer to bring yourself intentionally into the presence of God. Then read (or review) the pages marked from *Sensible Shoes*. Before pondering the questions, read the daily Scripture text (marked in bold in the exercises) so that your reflection is framed by the Word.

We each have stories that have shaped us. Some of them are painful to remember. But I believe with all my heart that God invites us to remember the stories and to see them as part of the larger picture of what he's weaving for us. Somehow—though we don't often see the "why" of it—the darker threads are part of the beauty.

The psalmist says, "Let the redeemed of the LORD tell their story" (Psalm 107:2).

May you have the courage to tell yours.

Sharon Garlough Brown

*May the Lord direct your hearts into God's love
and Christ's perseverance.*

(2 THESSALONIANS 3:5)

2

Reading for Week One: Chapter One

....

Week One: Day One

ↀ

CHAPTER ONE: INVITATION TO A JOURNEY
MEG (PP. 9-12, 36-39)

1. What details from Meg's story catch your attention? Do you sense any connection between her story and yours? If so, what are the common threads? The differences?

2. When the grown-up Meg crosses the threshold into her childhood house, everything has changed. Describe her sense of grief and loss. Have you ever found yourself crossing a "threshold" and asking a *Now what?* question? Spend some time remembering and recording the details in your journal.

3. **Read Psalm 107:1-9.** What are some of the "desert wastelands" you can already identify in Meg's life, just from these opening scenes? What is she hungry and thirsty for?

4. Identify some of the desert wastelands where you have wandered. What are you hungry and thirsty for?

Prayer: *Lord, I give you thanks for your unfailing love to me, even when I haven't been aware of it. Help me to cry out to you in my trouble and to trust you to lead me to a place of rest. Let me be satisfied with your love and presence. In Jesus' name.*

....

Week One: Day Two

CHAPTER ONE: INVITATION TO A JOURNEY
HANNAH (PP. 12-17, 24-28)

1. What details from Hannah's story catch your attention? Do you sense any connection between her story and yours? If so, what are the common threads? The differences?

2. Did you have a special confidant or safe haven as a child? What about as an adult? Where do you go with your secrets and heartaches?

3. Consider the rhythm and pace of your own life, your rhythm of work and rest. Have any of Pastor Steve's or Nancy's observations about Hannah ever been true about you? How might God be looking to "prune" you right now?

4. **Read Psalm 107:1-3, 10-16.** What are some of the "iron chains" you can already identify in Hannah's life, just from these opening scenes? Where is she captive and in darkness?

5. Using some words or images from Psalm 107, offer your heart to God.

....

Week One: Day Three

CHAPTER ONE: INVITATION TO A JOURNEY
MARA (PP. 17-20, 31-36)

1. What details from Mara's story catch your attention? Do you sense any connection between her story and yours? If so, what are the common threads? The differences?

2. Mara was never chosen by her peers. How is the theme of rejection echoed in her relationship with her husband and teenage sons? If you were Mara, how would you respond to Tom and the boys?

3. **Read Psalm 107:1-9.** What are some of the "desert wastelands" you can already identify in Mara's life, just from these opening scenes? What is she hungry and thirsty for?

4. Mara has a deep negative reaction to the description of the sacred journey. She hates the word *discipline* because she already feels guilty. What's your reaction when you hear the phrase *spiritual disciplines*? Does Dawn's example of the sun rising (p. 34) help you understand the process of transformation? Why or why not?

5. Using some words or images from Psalm 107, offer your longings to God.

....

Week One: Day Four

∽

CHAPTER ONE: INVITATION TO A JOURNEY
CHARISSA (PP. 21-24, 28-31)

1. What details from Charissa's story catch your attention? Do you sense any connection between her story and yours? If so, what are the common threads? The differences?

2. What things have shaped Charissa's sense of self? How have significant people in her life reinforced the message about what is important?

3. **Read Psalm 107:1-3, 10-16.** What are some of the "bars of iron" you can already identify in Charissa's life, just from these opening scenes? Where is she captive and in darkness?

4. What are the things that have shaped your sense of self? What messages have you received from others about what is important? In what ways have these events or messages become places of captivity for you?

5. Charissa's professor has been encouraging his students to find ways to deepen their life with God. What helps you pay attention to the "path and contours of your own spiritual journey" (p. 22)? What gets in the way of paying attention?

6. Using some words or images from Psalm 107, offer your longings to God.

Week One: Day Five

CHAPTER ONE: INVITATION TO A JOURNEY
SUMMARY

An invitation from New Hope:

Jesus says, "Are you tired? Worn out? Burned out on religion? Come to me. Get away with me and you'll recover your life. I'll show you how to take a real rest. Walk with me and work with me—watch how I do it. Learn the unforced rhythms of grace. I won't lay anything heavy or ill-fitting on you. Keep company with me and you'll learn to live freely and lightly" (**Matthew 11:28-30**, *The Message*). We invite you to come take a sacred journey.

The sacred journey is a pilgrimage for those who are thirsty for more of God. This journey is for all those who are dissatisfied with living on the surface and who want to travel deeper into God's heart. We invite you to come and explore spiritual disciplines as we seek to create sacred space for God.

1. This week you've been introduced to four characters through flashbacks and current experiences. Is there a particular flashback that stirs an emotional response with you? Why? In what ways do you think these childhood events may have affected the adult characters?

2. Each of the women has received an invitation to the New Hope Retreat Center. Each is resisting the invitation for different reasons. What is behind the resistance for each one? How are they encouraged or discouraged

from moving forward? Who or what encourages or discourages you from traveling deeper into the heart of God?

3. Spend some time thinking about words such as *thirst, dissatisfaction,* and *agitation.* How might God use these things to draw you to himself?

4. Jesus has invited you on a sacred journey with him. Write an RSVP note, naming the reasons why you are excited or why you aren't sure about accepting. Be honest about your hopes and fears. Offer your heart in prayer to God.

Week One Group Discussion

CHAPTER ONE: INVITATION TO A JOURNEY

Note from Sharon: One of the best gifts we can give one another in community is the promise of confidentiality. As you begin to walk together, commit to creating a safe place. Devote yourselves to being faithful stewards of one another's stories. Only then are we truly free to offer our authentic selves to one another, without fear of being judged or betrayed. As you continue to journey together, remind yourselves frequently of your commitment to each other. Pray for God to guard, protect, and establish you in your life together.

When you gather together, avoid the impulse to give advice, "fix," or commiserate ("I know just how you feel because something similar happened to me when . . ."). Give space to pregnant silence. Don't rush to fill the quiet, even if it feels uncomfortable or awkward. Trust that the Holy Spirit is stirring hearts in the midst of the silence and giving people the courage to speak. (This will be a particularly important gift to offer the introverts in your group.) Practice listening for the presence of God in both the silence and the words offered. Encourage one another to share from the heart, without compelling anyone to do so. Gently and lovingly remind one another to return to these practices of life together whenever you find yourself drifting off course.

You'll find suggested group questions at the end of each week in this guide, but feel free to modify them according to the needs and desires of your group. As you find your rhythm together, you may simply want to share in an open-ended way about what God is stirring as a result of your prayerful reflections during the week. Bring your journal to each session just in case there's something specific you want to share or record in it during your time together.

Intro: If the group hasn't been together before, offer introductions and ask, "What are you hoping for in this study together?"

1. Read Psalm 107:1-9. What are some of the "desert wastelands" you can already identify in Meg's life? In Mara's life? What have they been hungry and thirsty for? (From day one and day three.)

   What points of connection do you share with these characters?

2. Read Psalm 107:10-16. What are some of the "iron chains" you can already identify in Hannah's life? In Charissa's life? Where are they captive? (From day two and day four.)

   What points of connection do you share with these characters?

3. Using some of the day five questions as a launching point, discuss resistance and responsiveness to the invitation to travel deep into God's heart (both the characters' resistance or responses and your own). How do you feel about taking this journey with others?

4. If you're comfortable doing so, share your RSVP note with others in the group. How can you pray for one another as you begin to walk together?

5. Close your time of prayer by reading Matthew 11:28-30 (*The Message*) in unison:

   [Jesus says,] "Are you tired? Worn out? Burned out on religion? Come to me. Get away with me and you'll recover your life. I'll show you how to take a real rest. Walk with me and work with me—watch how I do it. Learn the unforced rhythms of grace. I won't lay anything heavy or ill-fitting on you. Keep company with me and you'll learn to live freely and lightly."

Reading for Week Two: Chapter Two

In preparation for day five, explore whether there are any local prayer labyrinths open to the public. (Try labyrinthlocator.com for locations.) Some churches and retreat centers offer canvas labyrinths for rental or have outdoor courtyards. If you're traveling with a group, you may decide to use your group time to walk a labyrinth together. Day five includes a note from Sharon about labyrinths.

....

Week Two: Day One

∞

CHAPTER TWO: THE PILGRIMAGE BEGINS
NEW HOPE (PP. 40-54)

1. As the "pilgrims" arrive at the New Hope Retreat Center and prepare to begin the journey, you are given access into Meg's, Mara's, and Hannah's points of view. Do you share anything in common with these women as you start a new adventure? With which character do you most identify? Least identify? Why?

2. Hannah is intrigued by testimonies on the New Hope website about what the sacred journey has meant to others: "The sacred journey helped me understand and navigate the landscape of my inner world so that I could walk more closely with God." "I started to see the things that move me toward God and away from God." "I grew, not only in intimacy with Christ, but in intimacy with my own self" (p. 50). Do any of these

testimonies intrigue you? Stir your longings? Make you anxious? What do you hope you'll say at the end of this study?

3. On page 51 Katherine Rhodes describes the spiritual life as a journey that requires slowness and attentiveness. What is the pace of your life? Do you tend to live on autopilot, or do you regularly take time to slow down and listen to God? How can you create more space to pay attention to the Holy Spirit and to others?

4. Katherine exhorts the pilgrims not to be afraid of the mess as they move forward in the journey toward transformation and freedom. How do you feel about mess and chaos? Have you ever experienced a loss of equilibrium or sense of disorientation in your life? Remember and record the circumstances. How do you trust God in the midst of mess?

5. **Read Psalm 84:5-7.** Using images from the psalm, offer your longings, hopes, and fears to God.

Week Two: Day Two

CHAPTER TWO: THE PILGRIMAGE BEGINS
A PATH FOR PRAYER (PP. 56-62)

1. The labyrinth provides an opportunity to slow down and pay attention to God in prayer. What does Hannah notice as she walks the labyrinth? Do you share anything in common with her?

2. What does the image of rushing in and out of God's presence to deliver flowers reveal about Hannah's relationship with God? Does this image speak to your life? Why or why not?

3. What distractions keep Charissa from engaging with the spiritual discipline of walking the labyrinth? Are you sympathetic to her frustrations? Why or why not?

4. **Read Luke 10:38-42.** Do you feel free to take your frustration, resentment, and irritation to Jesus, as Martha does, or do you stuff and hide your impolite impulses?

5. What tone of voice do you imagine Jesus using with Martha? With you?

6. What distracts and hinders you from sitting still in Jesus' presence and listening to what he says? What are some of the things you are "worried and upset about"? Offer these distractions and your longings to God in prayer.

....

Week Two: Day Three

CHAPTER TWO: THE PILGRIMAGE BEGINS
A PATH FOR PRAYER (PP. 62-69)

1. Meg is caught off guard by seemingly ordinary and innocuous things that trigger her grief, such as clearing dishes. Have you ever been surprised by a trigger point? Are you aware of what provokes deep emotional or spiritual responses in you? Spend some time naming and pondering both the triggers and your response.

2. Meg doesn't think she has anything profound to say or add to the group. She thinks the group might be too advanced for her. But Katherine says, "You begin the journey with a wonderful gift, Meg, if you already know you are poor in spirit—if you already see how desperately you need God.

Humility is always the starting place for those who want to draw near to God" (p. 63). Do you see being poor in spirit and being desperate for God as a gift? How poor and desperate do you feel right now? If you're feeling self-satisfied, begin to ask God for the gift of humility.

3. Katherine also explains that there is a "disabling sort of poverty that sneers you're never good enough, no matter what you do or how hard you try. The right kind of spiritual poverty is a pathway to seeing God; the other kind prevents you from seeing who God has created you to be" (p. 63). Do you ever feel hindered by the sneering, disabling kind of spiritual poverty Katherine describes? In what ways? Who do you believe God has created you to be?

4. **Read 2 Corinthians 12:9-10.** Have you experienced the reality of God's strength in the midst of your weakness? In what ways?

5. Katherine offers a breath prayer, a simple way of turning frequently to God. "I'll inhale saying the words, 'I can't' and exhale saying the words, 'You can, Lord,' over and over again throughout the day" (p. 64). Commit to breathing this simple prayer throughout the day. For now, take the prayer one step further and write down things you can't do, followed by "You can, Lord."

I can't _____. You can, Lord.

Notice how this rhythm of drawing your attention to your weakness and God's strength encourages you throughout the day.

....

Week Two: Day Four

CHAPTER TWO: THE PILGRIMAGE BEGINS
SUMMARY

1. Katherine says, "Navigating our external world is often a piece of cake compared to traveling the labyrinth of our inner world. . . . You're likely to experience distractions and confusion as you journey. There may be times when you'll feel discouraged and be tempted to give up. But if you persevere—if you press on in hope and confidence that the Lord himself is directing your journey and is with you as you travel—it will be a marvelous adventure. It's also a special gift to walk with trustworthy companions. We need each other. God doesn't want us traveling alone" (p. 61). How are you feeling about the journey so far? Are you experiencing any of Katherine's words to be true? Or, like Charissa, are you feeling skeptical or frustrated?

2. Hannah and Meg take a tentative first step toward community by going out to lunch together. If you're studying in a group, plan a time for fellowship outside of your regularly scheduled meeting. If you're using this study for personal devotion, pray about connecting with someone else for conversation and prayer. Who might God provide as a companion for you?

3. Katherine describes spiritual disciplines as "practices that help us cultivate a deeper attachment to Jesus." Disciplines provide ways "to create sacred space in our lives so we have more freedom to say yes to God" (p. 52). What is helping you to say yes to God right now? What is hindering you? How can you find ways to rest and enjoy God's deep love for you?

4. **Read Jeremiah 6:16.** Identify some "crossroads" moments in your life. How did you know which direction to go? What kind of guidance are you looking for right now? What practices help you to listen?

5. Offer your longings to God in prayer.

Week Two: Day Five

CHAPTER TWO: THE PILGRIMAGE BEGINS
A PATH FOR PRAYER (P. 55)

1. Turn to the path for prayer handout and read it slowly. Even if you aren't able to locate a full-sized labyrinth for walking in prayer, there are other ways to make a slow and intentional journey, using the rhythm of releasing, receiving, and returning. You may wish to print out a labyrinth pattern (available online) and trace the path with your finger or a pencil, pausing along the way to be still and listen. Or you can go on a prayer walk in your neighborhood or in a park. Just designate a halfway point where you can pause and dwell on the love of God before you return by the same path.

   Consider using **Matthew 11:28-30** as you pray. What heavy burdens are you carrying? What yokes are weighing you down? Spend some time naming and releasing these things as you journey toward the center. At the center or midpoint of your journey, receive Jesus' gift of rest. Invite him to bind you to himself with his easy yoke so that you might keep in step with him as you make your return.

2. Spend some time journaling about your experience. What did you notice as you slowed down to journey in prayer?

3. At the end of the first session, Katherine invites the pilgrims to consider their images of God: "Notice especially how your current images have taken shape and changed over the years. Who is God to you?" (p. 62). In preparation for next week's reflections, begin to think about your earliest

images of God. What shaped those images? What images of God are precious to you now? Why?

Note: Like Charissa, some Christians are nervous about labyrinths being a "New Age thing." Though some proponents of labyrinths believe that the pattern itself has mystical power and teach about how to achieve some kind of self-actualization through walking one, this is not a Christian viewpoint. (See Katherine's explanation, p. 53.) Texts such as Romans 14 and 1 Corinthians 8 can be helpful in any discussion about Christian freedom. Historically Christians have taken even pagan symbols and festivals and reinterpreted them in Christ (for example, the origin and celebration of Christmas). Paul offers this wisdom: "The faith that you have, have as your own conviction before God. Blessed are those who have no reason to condemn themselves because of what they approve. But those who have doubts are condemned if they eat, because they do not act from faith; for whatever does not proceed from faith is sin" (Romans 14:22-23 NRSV). Whether you choose to walk a labyrinth or abstain, do it "in honor of the Lord and give thanks to God" (Romans 14:6 NRSV).

Week Two Group Discussion

If you aren't walking a labyrinth together, use these questions to prompt group discussion.

1. Which character(s) did you find yourself identifying with this week? Why?

2. What is the pace of your life? How are you being invited to slow down? What are you noticing as you practice paying attention to the presence of God in new ways?

3. How are you feeling about the journey so far? What do you hope your testimony will be at the end of this study?

4. Is there a particular insight you'd like to share from your reflections this week? What stirred you?

5. Turn to Luke 10:38-42 and have a volunteer read it aloud. Listen for where you find yourself in the story. What is Jesus saying to you? With what tone of voice?

Conclude by inviting each person to name one way in which they'd like to be prayed for in the coming week. Close with silent prayer.

Reading for Week Three: Chapter Three

....

Week Three: Day One

∞

CHAPTER THREE: EXPLORING THE HEART OF GOD
MARA (PP. 70-74, 89-93)

1. As Mara walked and prayed on the labyrinth, she was flooded by painful memories from her past. What feelings arise for you as you read the details of her pain? Are there any points of connection between your story and Mara's?

2. Mara finds it difficult to believe that Jesus has chosen her. But her counselor, Dawn, says, "Jesus *has* chosen you, Mara. You weren't just the leftover God had to take, simply because you were standing there. God didn't choose you out of pity. Jesus really has chosen you to be with him because he loves you and wants to be with you" (p. 91). Do you believe Jesus has chosen you because he loves you and wants to be with you? What difference does it make (or would it make) to truly believe that?

3. Mara is haunted by guilt, shame, regret, and a deep sense of condemnation. Even her image of God has shifted from *El Roi*, the God who saw her with compassion, to *El Roi*, the God who watches her with judgment. How does

God see you? How do you see yourself? Is there anything from your past that continues to haunt you? What steps is God inviting you to take?

4. **Read Ephesians 1:3-12** slowly. If you were alongside Mara as a friend, what words or phrases from the text would you offer to her as encouragement? What words or phrases is the Holy Spirit offering to you as encouragement?

5. Offer your hopes and longings to God in prayer.

....

Week Three: Day Two

CHAPTER THREE: EXPLORING THE HEART OF GOD
CHARISSA (PP. 74-82)

1. Dr. Allen says, "The things that annoy, irritate, and disappoint us have just as much power to reveal the truth about ourselves as anything else. Learn to linger with what provokes you. You may just find the Spirit of God moving there" (p. 80). What's provoking Charissa? Are you provoked by any similar things?

2. Charissa is accustomed to people seeing only what she wants them to see, and now Dr. Allen sees something about her that she has yet to perceive about herself. Have you ever experienced anyone seeing you more clearly than you desire? How do you feel about being seen? How do you feel about seeing yourself more clearly?

3. What do you notice about how Charissa approaches God's Word, both in her personal study time and in her reflections about her images of God? Do you share anything in common with her?

4. Dr. Allen says, "Much as we might wish to direct our own spiritual journeys, growing in love for God and others is a lifelong process that can't be achieved by self-effort. We've got to learn how to cooperate with the Holy Spirit" (p. 81). Which image better describes your spiritual journey—sailboat or motorboat? Why?

5. Charissa hears Dr. Allen's words as a rebuke. Have you ever experienced a loving rebuke from someone you respected? How did you respond?

6. **Read Revelation 3:17-20** aloud. What words or images from the text connect with Charissa's life? What words or images connect with your life? What words of loving correction and discipline is Jesus offering to you? How do you respond?

7. Speak to Jesus about what you have noticed. Listen for his invitation, compassion, and grace.

. . . .

Week Three: Day Three

CHAPTER THREE: EXPLORING THE HEART OF GOD
HANNAH (PP. 82-89)

1. Why does Hannah find it hard to rest? Is deep rest easy or difficult for you? Why?

2. What is Hannah grieving? Do you share anything in common with her grief points?

3. Hannah's first image of God was a Father who fixed things. This image mirrored her earthly father. What was your first image of God? Did that image mirror anyone in your life?

4. Have you ever had an image of God die? If so, what was the image? Was it a true or false image of God? How did (or will) you process the loss?

5. As she reflects on the scenes of sorrow she has witnessed in her pastoral role, Hannah begins to see that she has slowly and quietly come to be disappointed with God. Have you ever felt disappointed with God? What were the circumstances that brought about those feelings? How did (or will) you talk with God about it?

6. **Read Psalm 42.** What images speak to you personally right now? Write your own version of the psalm and offer it as prayer to God.

··

Week Three: Day Four

CHAPTER THREE: EXPLORING THE HEART OF GOD
MEG (PP. 93-98)

1. How have Meg's losses affected her? Why is she so afraid? Can you identify with any of her fears?

2. Meg internalized many negative messages from her mother that affected the way she viewed herself. What negative messages have you internalized over the years? Who has God used to help you hear the truth about who he is and who you are?

3. As she continues to pray, Meg lets her mind consider some "what if" questions. "What if she really believed she belonged to Jesus? What if the shepherd really did come and find her when she felt lost and afraid? What if the assurance of his presence really was enough to strengthen her and give her courage?" (pp. 96-97). Answer Meg's questions for yourself. Then add any other "what if" questions that come to mind. Offer these to God in prayer.

4. Though Meg has always viewed her imagination as a liability, Katherine invites her to see it as a gift. "Jesus also had a wonderful imagination," Katherine tells her. "He had an amazing way of inviting listeners to enter his stories and catch glimpses of who God is" (p. 98). **Read Psalm 23**, and spend some time picturing yourself walking with the Good Shepherd. What images spring to life for you? How is the Word becoming flesh as you ponder it, imagine it, and pray it? Talk with the Good Shepherd about what you notice.

....

Week Three: Day Five

∞

CHAPTER THREE: EXPLORING THE HEART OF GOD
HANNAH (PP. 98-101)

1. When Hannah arrives at New Hope for the second session, she observes that several people have not returned. "Hannah wasn't surprised. Intense and prayerful introspection wasn't for the fainthearted" (p. 99). How are

you feeling about the journey so far? As you practice paying attention, are you surprised by anything you're seeing about yourself or God?

2. "Though Hannah knew many people thoroughly and intimately, very few knew her" (p. 101). Do you share anything in common with her? Have you erected any "No Trespassing" signs around your own life? Does God have unlimited access to the deepest places of your heart? Why or why not?

3. **Read Matthew 16:15**, then read the following images for God aloud slowly. Notice which words attract or repel you. Do any of them draw you in or make you uncomfortable? If an image stirs a strong response in you, ask the Holy Spirit to show you why. Then spend some time journaling about your response.

   Jesus. Savior. Lord. Creator. Father. Provider. Healer. Spirit. Revealer. Good Shepherd. Lover. Physician. Tower. Rock. Door. Wind. Light of the World. Living Water. Teacher. Friend. Comforter. Counselor. I AM. Guide. Helper. Victor. Rescuer. Truth. Way. Immanuel. Redeemer. Artist. Author. Word. Treasure. King. Lamb. Host. Hiding Place. Love. Vine. Fire. Gardener. Builder. Resurrection. Life.

4. Using your own images for God or words from this list, write a prayer that expresses your desire to know and trust God as he is portrayed in that image. For example, if your image is "Redeemer," what does it mean for you to know God as Redeemer? What comfort or challenge comes to you when you seek God as Redeemer?

Week Three Group Discussion

CHAPTER THREE: EXPLORING THE HEART OF GOD

1. Which character(s) did you find yourself identifying with this week? Why? Did any of them provoke you? Why?

2. What were some of your earliest images of God? How have these images changed over the years? What brought about the changes?

3. Which images of God are precious to you now?

4. What insights would you like to share with the group from your own reflections this week? What are you noticing about your life with God?

5. Read Ephesians 1:3-12 several times aloud, listening for words, phrases, or images that catch your attention. What encouragement do you hear in this text? What encouragement do you need to hear from someone else? Spend some time encouraging one another and praying for God to encourage you in the journey.

Reading for Week Four:
Chapters Four and Five

In preparation for day four, you'll need a simple pillar candle to use as a Christ candle.

....

Week Four: Day One

∞

CHAPTER FOUR: LEARNING TO LINGER
LECTIO DIVINA (PP. 102-107)

1. Turn to the handout on lectio divina (p. 102) and read it aloud. Then think about how you approach reading the Bible. Do you read quickly, skimming for main ideas? Do you look for what you get out of it instead of allowing the Word to get into you? Do you try to control the process of reading Scripture, or do you yield to the supernatural revealing of the Holy Spirit? What is it like for you to slow down and read a text out loud?

2. Why does Charissa struggle with this spiritual discipline? What is provoking her? Do you identify with Charissa? If so, in what way?

3. Katherine says, "Picture lectio divina as a way of feasting on God's Word. First we take a bite; then we chew, savoring the taste of it; and finally we swallow and digest it, and it becomes part of us" (pp. 103-104). Slowly read the text from **John 1:35-39** out loud. Listen for a word or phrase

that catches your attention and invites you to linger with it. Don't analyze it. Just listen to it. Give yourself some silent space before you read the text aloud again. Then begin to ponder why this particular word or phrase is speaking to you. How does it connect with your life?

4. Read the text aloud a third time. Listen for God's invitation to you. Then begin a conversation with God. What do you want to say to God about what you are hearing? How does the text lead you into prayerful dialogue with God?

5. Finally, read the text aloud one more time. Then simply rest in God's presence. No words are necessary. Just be still and know that he is God.

....

Week Four: Day Two

∽

CHAPTER FOUR: LEARNING TO LINGER
DRAWING NEAR (PP. 107-115)

1. Using the method of lectio divina, prayerfully read **John 1:35-39** and journal what is coming to life and light as you listen.

2. Both Meg and Hannah are struggling to answer the question, "What are you looking for?" Why? Do you share anything in common with either of them?

3. Imagine Jesus turning and looking at you. He asks you, "What are you looking for?" How do you respond?

....

Week Four: Day Three

∞

CHAPTER FIVE: COME AND SEE
MARA (PP. 116-121)

1. After listening to a sermon about Moses meeting God at the burning bush, Mara decides to pay attention to what God might be revealing to her by meeting privately with Katherine. What is she struggling with? Do you share anything in common with her? If you believe God has expectations for you, what are they?

2. Katherine says, "God knows your weaknesses. Your frailty. Your imperfections. Your sin. Your humanity. And if nothing about you takes God by surprise, what expectations are you disappointing?" (p. 119). Do you

agree with Katherine that it is impossible to disappoint God? Why or why not?

3. Mara sees her sin and hears a belittling, accusing, shaming, and condemning voice. Why can't she "get rid of the guilt" (p. 120)? What does Katherine suggest she do? How might these practices benefit you as well?

4. Are you convinced that God is love? Do you see yourself as God's beloved? What voices are you listening to?

5. Have you ever told the whole truth about your life to someone else? What was that experience like for you? How has that experience shaped you? What do you want or need to say to God about that?

6. Do you sense the Holy Spirit hovering over your life and speaking new realities into being? If so, what?

7. **Read John 1:35-39.** Jesus invites the disciples to "come and see." Imagine yourself going to Jesus and remaining with him. What would

you like to see? Is there anything you are afraid you might see? Offer your longings and fears to God in prayer.

....

Week Four: Day Four

⚬⚬

CHAPTER FIVE: COME AND SEE
HANNAH (PP. 121-128)

At the beginning of the spiritual direction session with Hannah, Katherine lights a candle symbolizing Christ's presence to remind them they are in the presence of the Holy One. She prays, "Jesus Christ, Light of the World, come and light the dark corners of our lives. Where we are blind, grant us sight. Where we stumble in darkness, illumine our path. Quiet us with your love, and enable us to hear your still, small voice. For you are our dear friend, Lord, and we long to be fully present to you" (p. 122).

Light a Christ candle. Slowly pray the prayer above, making it your own. You may wish to continue this practice each day as you begin your time of reflection.

1. What images does Hannah use to describe what her life feels like? Have you ever felt like Hannah? In what way?

2. What images or passages from Scripture come to mind to describe what your life feels like right now?

3. Hannah describes the "false self" as "all the ways we wrap our identities around how much we achieve, or how well we perform, or what other people think of us" (p. 125). What other "secondary things" can become sources of significance and identity? Which of these has been a source of identity or temptation for you?

4. Katherine says, "Jesus loves you too much to let you root your identity in what you do for him, rather than who you are to him. He loves you too much to let you wrap yourself in anything other than his love for you— his deep, uncontainable, extravagant love for you" (p. 125). What keeps you from embracing the identity that you are the one Jesus loves? What helps you to embrace that identity? Which is easier for you: to name that as an identity for others, or to receive it for yourself? Why?

5. **Read John 1:35-39** once more. What are you seeing as you take time to remain with Jesus? How do you feel about what you see? Offer these observations and feelings to the God who sees you, knows you, and loves you.

Week Four: Day Five

∞

CHAPTER FIVE: COME AND SEE
HANNAH (PP. 121-128; SAME READING AS DAY FOUR)

1. When Hannah meets Mara and Meg at the labyrinth (pp. 127-128), Mara describes a shift that seems to be happening in her perspective. What is she beginning to see about the way God sees her? Why is this significant?

2. Like Mara, Hannah also struggles to receive the extravagance of God's love. When Hannah begins to see the truth about how she has wrapped her life around her work as a source of significance, Katherine reassures her that God is not condemning or punishing her. "This is his love, pursuing you and enfolding you, tenderly drawing you near to heal and restore" (p. 125). How do you see God? How does God see you? Do you believe God's desires for you are rooted in love and longing for you, or in disappointment and condemnation? Why?

3. What Scripture texts help you focus on God's love for you?

4. Hannah describes both the death of her first image of God and the death of her image of herself. How do these deaths open up the possibility for something new to be born? What about for you? What is dying and what is being born? Does it encourage or discourage you to think about dying to sin and self and then rising again to new life as a lifelong process?

5. When Hannah names her discomfort with the image of God as Lover, Katherine comments, "Stay with what stirs you. Our areas of resistance and avoidance can provide a wealth of information about our inner life. Don't be afraid to go deep" (p. 127). What's stirring you right now? What are you resisting or avoiding? Are you afraid of going deep? What is the Holy Spirit revealing? Are you paying attention?

6. **Read Romans 8:31-39.** Then make your own list of things that do not— and can never—separate you from the love of God in Jesus Christ. What do you say in response to this promise from God to you?

Week Four Group Discussion

If you have a Christ candle, light it as you begin your time together. Open with a unison prayer: "Jesus Christ, Light of the World, come and light the dark corners of our lives. Where we are blind, grant us sight. Where we stumble in darkness, illumine our path. Quiet us with your love, and enable us to hear your still, small voice. For you are our dear friend, Lord, and we long to be fully present to you."

1. Lectio divina: Choose four different readers to read the Scripture text out loud (John 1:35-39). Allow for several minutes of silence between each reading.

2. *First reading:* Listen for a word or phrase that catches your attention and invites you to ponder it. Don't analyze it. Simply listen for something that speaks more loudly than the other words.

3. *After the second reading:* Begin to chew on the word or phrase that caught your attention. What connection does it have with your life right now? Pay attention to any particular emotions that arise with that word or phrase.

4. *After the third reading:* Speak with God about what you're noticing, hearing, or feeling. What might God want to say to you in response?

5. *After the fourth reading:* Give yourselves some silence to just rest in the presence of God. Then spend time privately recording in your journal what you noticed. After fifteen to twenty minutes (or longer if you need it), share what you heard from the text as you listened prayerfully. What is the Holy Spirit stirring in you?

6. What other "aha" moments would you like to share from your reflections this week?

7. Is there anything you're wrestling with right now? How can the group pray for you?

Reading for Week Five:
Chapters Five and Six

From this point forward, you are invited to continue a daily practice of lectio divina with the Scripture texts offered.

....

Week Five: Day One

CHAPTER FIVE: COME AND SEE
MEG (PP. 128-132)

1. Describe the voices Meg has been listening to. Whose voices have shaped you over the years, positively and negatively? What messages have you internalized? What message do you need to hear right now?

2. As Meg meditates on God's love for her, she feels like she is awakening from deep sleep. She begins to recognize the Good Shepherd's voice. "You are [the one] I love. You're safe. I have found you. You are mine" (p. 132). Imagine Jesus speaking these words to you. What is your response? How are you awakening to the ways God loves and treasures you?

3. Answers to the questions, Who am I? and, What do I want? are beginning to emerge for Meg. How do you answer those questions?

4. **Read John 10:2-5.** What is your prayer?

....

Week Five: Day Two

∞

CHAPTER FIVE: COME AND SEE
CHARISSA (PP. 132-142)

1. How does Charissa's story connect with the story of Nicodemus in **John 3:1-9**? How is she "in the dark"? How is Jesus unsettling her? What does she need to unlearn?

2. Dr. Allen speaks a painfully hard word to Charissa, identifying her idols of learning, control, perfectionism, and trying to be good apart from Jesus. What idols (anything that is more important to you than God) keep you from entrusting yourself wholeheartedly to Jesus?

SENSIBLE SHOES STUDY GUIDE

3. Dr. Allen tries to reassure Charissa that he isn't condemning or accusing her. He sees her struggles because as a perfectionist he has the same ones. "It's hard for a good rule follower to be converted to grace. . . . It's not your goodness that saves you. Or your performance. It's grace. All grace. And God wants to soften your heart and open your eyes so that you see how desperately you need that grace" (p. 137). Have you been radically converted to grace, or do you still stumble over the cross by trying to be good? Are you quick to acknowledge your sin and your need for grace, or do you hide behind your attempts to live a good life?

4. If you were Charissa, how would you react to Dr. Allen's hard word?

5. Read John 3:1-9 again. How does your story connect with the story of Nicodemus? Are you in the dark? Unsettled? Provoked? Confused? Take some time to linger with what provokes you and ask God to help you see. Offer your irritation, anger, confusion, and worries to God in prayer.

Week Five: Day Three

CHAPTER SIX: HIDING AND SEEKING
MEG (PP. 143-150)

1. Meg decides to open up her box of grief and look at everything she hid away. Do you have a box of grief that is unopened and locked away? What would give you courage to open it?

2. As Meg looks at her past, she wrestles with some "if only" regrets. When you look at your past, do you have any "if only" regrets? As you become aware of regrets, offer them to God in prayer.

3. When Meg asks Katherine how to know what she should do, Katherine replies, "One of the early church fathers wrote that the glory of God is revealed in a person who is fully alive" (p. 147). What makes you feel fully alive? What are the deep desires and longings of your heart? How might the glory of God be revealed in you and through you? Offer these desires and longings to God in prayer and listen for his response.

4. Meg is trying to get rid of her fears, and Katherine offers a shift in perspective (p. 149). What's your response to Katherine's words? Do you

tend to focus on your fears or on God's faithfulness? What attributes of God help you to trust him when you are afraid?

5. Katherine tells Meg that her fears can become opportunities for encountering Jesus in deeper intimacy, and she encourages Meg to listen prayerfully to what her fears are revealing (p. 148). Spend some time "listening to your fears." What do they reveal about who you are and how you need God? Then offer your fears to God in prayer.

6. **Read Isaiah 43:1-4** several times. Then personalize the verses, inserting your own name into the text. Write these verses on an index card and carry them with you, praying them frequently throughout the day.

....

Week Five: Day Four

∞

CHAPTER SIX: HIDING AND SEEKING
CHARISSA (pp. 150-156)

1. What patterns of sin do you notice in Charissa? Do you share any of the same patterns of sin? If so, what are they?

2. How does her sin affect her relationships? How does your sin affect your relationships?

3. Emily talks with Charissa about how she is growing through a spiritual formation group at her church. How has Emily experienced freedom? Is that kind of freedom frightening or attractive to you? Why?

4. Do you have an internal "toxic waste container" with a doily on top? What have you shoved inside of it? Are you afraid to open it? Why?

5. Emily says, "We all have this tendency to stuff and hide our darker sides— to think, 'Good Christian girls shouldn't feel that, shouldn't think that, shouldn't do that'" (p. 153). What have you told yourself you shouldn't do, think, or feel because you're a Christian? Rather than stuffing, hiding, and self-regulating, begin to confess your sin and receive God's grace.

6. What is Charissa afraid of? Do you share any fears in common?

7. **Read Psalm 32:1-4** slowly. Have you ever experienced the heavy hand of God trying to get your attention? What word of mercy and invitation do you hear in these verses? How do you respond?

Week Five: Day Five

CHAPTER SIX: HIDING AND SEEKING
SUNDAY (PP. 156-159)

1. Read each of the Sunday snapshots. What evidence of freedom do you
    see? What patterns of avoidance or captivity do you see? How is each of
    the women traveling (or not traveling) from fear to love?

2. Mara experiences a sacred moment on the playground (p. 159). What
    does God reveal to her? In what ways is she healed? Have you ever expe-
    rienced a sacred moment of encountering God in an unexpected place?
    If so, what was that like for you?

3. "No matter where you hide, I'll always find you. You belong to me, and I
    love you very, very much" (p. 159). How is Love seeking and finding you?

4. **Read Ezekiel 34:11-12, 15-16.** Use words or images from the text to
    offer your heart to God.

Week Five Group Discussion

Chapter Five: Come and See; Chapter Six: Hiding and Seeking

From now on, a text will be provided for group lectio divina each week. You can use the guide from week four in your practice together.

1. Read Isaiah 43:1-4 using lectio divina. What is the Holy Spirit revealing or stirring as you listen?

2. How are the characters traveling (or not traveling) from fear to love? What about you?

3. Which character(s) are you identifying with? Frustrated with? Why?

4. Are there any other "aha" moments you'd like to share from this week's reflections?

5. Offer one thing the group can pray for you this week.

Reading for Week Six:
Chapters Six and Seven

....

Week Six: Day One

∞

CHAPTER SIX: HIDING AND SEEKING
CHARISSA (PP. 159-165)

1. Why does Charissa decide to apologize to Dr. Allen? What motivates you to apologize? Have you ever avoided offering a full and sincere apology? What were you protecting?

2. Dr. Allen asks, "What troubles you about what you've seen in yourself?" (p. 162). How would you answer his question? Are you ever "disappointed by your own imperfection"?

3. What's the difference between self-centered repentance and God-centered repentance?

4. What do you notice about how Charissa confesses her sin to John? How is she moving from fear to love? What evidence do you see of the Holy Spirit's work in her life?

5. "Sin impacts our communion and intimacy with God and with other people" (pp. 162-163). Are there any relationships being impacted by your sin right now? What steps could you take toward restoring communion and intimacy?

6. **Read Psalm 32:5-10** slowly and prayerfully. What invitation or encouragement do you hear from God? How do you respond?

....

Week Six: Day Two

∞

CHAPTER SIX: HIDING AND SEEKING
HANNAH (PP. 165-174)

1. What inconsistencies do you notice between what Hannah teaches others and what she lives herself? Why do you think there's such a disconnect between her words and her actions? Do you notice any inconsistencies in your own life?

2. What further evidence do you see of Meg and Charissa moving from fear to love? What about Hannah?

3. Think about what you've learned about Hannah's life up until this chapter. How have some of her childhood experiences shaped her? Do you see any connections between your past experiences and a current experience of resistance or fear?

4. Charissa tells the others what she has learned from Dr. Allen about paying attention to the things that make her angry, defensive, or upset. When something bothers you, are you paying attention? What are you learning?

5. How can others in the body of Christ help you? Have you ever been hurt by a fellow Christian? Who do you trust with the deepest places of your heart?

6. **Read 1 John 4:18** slowly. How are you moving from fear to love? Offer your longings to God in prayer.

Week Six: Day Three

CHAPTER SIX: HIDING AND SEEKING
MARA (PP. 174-177)

1. Mara is able to name some of the wells she has drunk from over the years: material possessions, sexual gratification, approval, and acceptance. None of them kept her from being thirsty. What wells have you drawn from? What are you thirsty for?

2. What does it mean to drink from the well of Living Water? Are you satisfied with Jesus? Why or why not?

3. Mara has always seen herself as the leftover one God had to take just because she was standing there. "But what if Jesus chose her because he actually loved her and wanted her to be with him? What if Jesus chose her, not because he felt sorry for her, but because her life was precious to him? What if she was actually worth something to God?" (p. 177). How do you see yourself? Ask yourself Mara's "what if" questions:

   • What if Jesus chose you because he actually loves you and wants you to be with him?

   • What if he chose you, not because he felt sorry for you, but because your life is precious to him?

- What if he chose you because you are worth something to God?

- How would your life be different if you truly believed you are chosen, loved, significant, and precious?

4. Spend some time praying with the story in **John 4:4-15**. What do you want to say to Jesus?

....

Week Six: Day Four

CHAPTER SEVEN: WALKING ATTENTIVELY
THE EXAMEN (PP. 178-183)

1. Spend some time practicing the palms-up, palms-down prayer. What's distracting or worrying you right now? What do you need to receive from God?

2. At first Charissa is ready to dismiss her discomfort with the prayer exercise as a "wrist thing." Then she remembers the invitation to pay attention to what provokes her. How quick are you to dismiss the things that provoke you as insignificant or inconsequential? Is this way of praying helpful or agitating to you? Why?

3. Charissa realizes that "letting go takes practice." So does receiving. Which is more difficult for you? Why? How are you practicing releasing and receiving?

4. Now that Charissa is seeing her sin more clearly and confessing it more readily, another realization hits her. What does she want? Do you identify with her stronghold or her frustration?

5. Hannah also struggles with the prayer time. Why? Do you identify with her?

6. Are you comfortable with silence? Why or why not? Why is silence an important spiritual discipline? If you don't regularly practice silence, try to incorporate it into the rhythm of your life by creating brief spaces for undistracted quiet. Gradually increase the time you spend sitting still and quietly listening. What do you notice?

7. **Read 1 Peter 5:7.** Practice the palms-up, palms-down prayer again. This time, as you put your palms down pray, "Cast all your cares on him." As you put your palms up pray, "for he cares for you." What encouragement does this verse give you?

....

Week Six: Day Five

∞

CHAPTER SEVEN: WALKING ATTENTIVELY
THE EXAMEN (PP. 178-183)

1. Katherine names the examen as one of her most important daily disciplines. Why?

2. Katherine says, "In the examen we ask the Spirit to search us and know us. The Lord invites us to perceive his constant activity in our lives, to notice the things that move us toward God and away from God. This kind of praying takes us deeply inward—not so we become self-absorbed and self-centered, but so that we can truly know ourselves. After all, self-knowledge and humility are pathways to knowing and loving God more and more" (p. 182). As you take time to prayerfully ponder your

life with God, are you becoming more self-absorbed and self-centered or more receptive and open to loving God and others? In what ways?

3. **Read Psalm 139:23-24.** Then turn to the handout on the prayer of examen (p. 178) and begin practicing this as a daily spiritual discipline. (Try praying it as an evening discipline.) Use the full version today and as often as possible. On days when you are rushed or tired, simplify the prayer by asking two questions: When was I aware of and responsive to God today? When was I unaware of or unresponsive to God today? Confess what needs to be confessed and receive God's grace and forgiveness. Watch for any particular patterns or themes that emerge as you pray. Remember to keep track of what you're noticing in your journal.

Week Six Group Discussion

1. Open with the palms-up, palms-down prayer, casting your cares on Jesus and receiving his care for you. Pay attention to any resistance toward letting go or receiving. Offer your longings and resistance to God in prayer.

2. Read John 4:4-15 using lectio divina. What is the Holy Spirit stirring in you as you pray with this text?

3. Which characters are you identifying with? Why? What are you learning about yourself as you watch them struggle and grow?

4. Are there any other insights you'd like to share from this week? How can the group pray for you?

Commit to practicing the examen in the coming week. Come next week prepared to share some of what you're noticing as you use the examen.

Reading for Week Seven: Chapter Seven

Week Seven: Day One

CHAPTER SEVEN: WALKING ATTENTIVELY
TOGETHER (PP. 184-191)

1. As Meg tells the others a bit about her family, she realizes how disconnected she is from her own history. Have you ever told someone your story and been surprised by their deep and compassionate reaction? If so, what did that experience unlock for you?

2. At Hannah's urging and manipulation, Mara opens up to the others about her past. Though she experiences compassion and understanding from Meg, she suffers silent but visible judgment and condemnation from Charissa. Have you ever told your story to someone else and experienced rejection? How have you prayed through that experience, or how is God inviting you to offer it to him now?

3. Charissa has spent her life avoiding people like Mara, unwilling to be guilty by association. Her mother always told her, "If you lose your reputation, you lose everything" (p. 184). What reputation did Jesus have?

What reputation do you have? How important is your reputation to you, and how have you worked to improve, protect, or maintain it? What has a commitment to defend your reputation cost you in your relationships?

4. "The spiritual life is a journey, not an exam." Which image do you tend to use when thinking about your own spiritual life: journey or exam? Why?

5. **Read Mark 2:13-17** slowly. Do you tend to think of yourself as healthy or sick? Righteous or sinner? How does this view of yourself impact your sense of need and longing for Jesus? Offer your reflections to him in prayer.

Remember to use the prayer of examen this week as an end-of-the-day reflection. Keep track of what you notice as you pray.

Week Seven: Day Two

∞

CHAPTER SEVEN: WALKING ATTENTIVELY
MEG (PP. 191-195)

1. Meg grew up in a troubled family where she internalized the message, "Don't you dare take this out of the house!" Did you grow up with a burden of shame or secrecy about what happened in your house? How free are you to tell the truth about your struggles now?

2. Meg receives the gift of a memory of her father, triggered by a walk down the steps at the beach. Have you ever remembered something that surprised you? What were the circumstances of that memory emerging? Was the memory a gift or a burden to you?

3. What are you most grateful for? Spend some time thanking God for these good gifts.

4. "For some of you," Katherine had said, "it will be easier to review the times when you were aware of God's presence. It will be easier to name the moments when you experienced joy, love, and peace. You may be reluctant to confront the difficult struggles and darker feelings, but God is present in all of life. . . . Don't be afraid of asking what God is saying through the things you'd rather overlook and ignore" (p. 194). Why is Meg reluctant to open more boxes of grief? Does the journey toward transformation and healing ever seem too long, too hard, too treacherous, or too frightening to you? What promises of God give you courage to persevere?

5. Imagine yourself as a child holding on to your Heavenly Father's hand. "I've got you," God says. "Keep coming." How do you need God's comfort and strength right now?

6. **Read Zephaniah 3:16-17** several times, receiving God's strengthening power and quieting love.

Week Seven: Day Three

∞

CHAPTER SEVEN: WALKING ATTENTIVELY
HANNAH AND MARA (PP. 195-199)

1. Hannah has been practicing a daily discipline of lectio divina through the Gospel of John. How does the Holy Spirit bring the wedding at Cana story (John 2) to life for her? What does meditating on this text reveal to her about where she is with God? How honest is she in her praying?

2. Do you share anything in common with Hannah's feelings and struggles?

3. As Mara prayerfully reviews the details of her day, she sees how quickly she has shifted from gratitude to self-doubt and negativity. What causes her spiral into sorrow and regret? Do you identify with the way Mara feels?

4. Both Hannah and Mara find themselves battling sorrow and regret. Does your past ever return to haunt you? Do you live with regret over major decisions you have made? Have you been able to talk with God about your "if onlys"?

5. **Read Psalm 139:1-12** aloud. Then use imagery from the psalm to express your heart to God.

Week Seven: Day Four

∞

CHAPTER SEVEN: WALKING ATTENTIVELY
HANNAH (PP. 199-201)

1. Hannah begins to identify her disappointment with herself, with her life, and even with God. Have you ever experienced profound disappointment with God? Are you able to name the reasons why?

2. Do you put a lot of energy into faking it? What keeps you from being authentic with others, yourself, and God?

3. Read Hannah's prayer of lament slowly. Have you ever felt this way about God? Have you talked to God this bluntly? Would you be afraid to? Why or why not?

4. Read Job's prayer of lament in **Job 7:11-20** slowly. Hear God's invitation to tell the truth. What do you need to say to God? Write your own prayer of lament to God.

. . . .

Week Seven: Day Five

∽

CHAPTER SEVEN: WALKING ATTENTIVELY
Summary

1. Meg speaks about her spiritual growth, saying, "Sometimes I feel like I'm not getting very far. Or like I'm traveling around in circles. Then I look back at where I've come from, and I guess I should feel encouraged" (p. 184). Do you ever feel like Meg? Take some time to read through your journal entries up until now. What encourages you about the direction you're traveling in?

2. Mara says to Meg, "I thought I was the only one who felt that way! I get dizzy, walkin' around in circles" (p. 184). How are you experiencing the truth that you are not alone? That your struggles are not uncommon? How is community a gift to you right now?

3. It has been said, "The truth will set you free, but first it will make you miserable." How is the truth making you miserable right now? How are you tasting freedom by seeing and naming the truth?

4. List some words of truth from God's Word that give you hope to persevere when you feel weary and discouraged. Are you living in the truth that you belong to God and that he loves you? In what ways?

5. What is the prayer of examen revealing to you as you practice it?

6. **Meditate on John 8:32.** Offer your fears, hopes, and longings to God in prayer.

Week Seven Group Discussion

CHAPTER SEVEN: WALKING ATTENTIVELY

1. Read Zephaniah 3:16-17 using lectio divina. What are you noticing as you listen to this text in prayer?

2. What insights emerged as you practiced the prayer of examen this week?

3. Which characters do you find yourself identifying with this week? Frustrated by? Why?

4. How comfortable are you with offering lament for others? For yourself? What about hearing others lament? If you feel comfortable, share some images or insights from the lament prayer you wrote (day four).

5. Name one way that your fellow pilgrims can help you walk in freedom and truth.

Reading for Week Eight:
Chapters Eight and Nine

Week Eight: Day One

∞

CHAPTER EIGHT: INTIMACY AND ENCOUNTER
CHARISSA (PP. 202-208)

1. Dr. Allen uses "Love (III)," a seventeenth-century poem by George Herbert, to invite his students to contemplate "the dance of movement between the soul and God, the movement of attraction and resistance" (p. 203). What does Charissa notice in her spirit as she listens both to the poem and to her classmates' observations?

2. In what ways can you identify with Charissa and her revelations? What kind of host are you to Jesus?

3. Is your life with God about grace or performance? Duty or love? Self-sufficiency or need? Why?

4. Dr. Allen says, "God is always the first one to move in his relationship with us. Our movement is always a response to the Love which loved us first. It's not about being more perfect in your faith or in your love for Jesus, Charissa—it's about being more open to responding to his deep love for you. So no guilt or condemnation about not seeing things before now, okay? It's the Spirit who opens the eyes of the blind. Always at the right time" (p. 206). How is Love bidding you welcome, drawing near, and tenderly reassuring you? Describe what it means for you to respond to the Love that loved you first.

5. Charissa has an "aha" moment about spirituality being all about intimacy—intimacy without defenses. Do you have any defenses against intimacy with others? With God? What are they?

6. Slowly **read Luke 7:36-50**. What is the connection between recognizing sin and loving God? How is the recognition of your sin and need for grace enlarging your heart for Jesus? What do you want to say to God?

Week Eight: Day Two

CHAPTER EIGHT: INTIMACY AND ENCOUNTER
HANNAH (PP. 209-211)

1. Hannah turns to her journal again after days of silence. She isn't talking to God, she won't call anyone in Chicago, and she won't tell Meg the truth about her crisis of faith. Why? Have you ever felt that kind of isolation? What do you do when you feel cut off from others or from God?

2. How does Hannah turn toward God, even when she isn't speaking to him?

3. What gifts does Katherine offer Hannah in their time together? What gifts do you need someone to offer you right now?

4. Are you an "internal bleeder"? What is taking up sacred space in your spirit right now? How might the emptying out of "accumulated toxicity" prepare you to receive something new?

5. Do you believe that expressing anger to God is a sign of intimacy with him? Why or why not? Do you trust God enough to offer him uncensored prayers?

6. **Read Psalm 43:2-3.** Using words or images from the text, offer your honest, uncensored prayer to God.

....

Week Eight: Day Three

CHAPTER EIGHT: INTIMACY AND ENCOUNTER
HANNAH (PP. 211-221)

1. Think about what you've learned so far about Dr. Nathan Allen and his commitment to tell the truth to Charissa and Hannah, even when it hurts. What difference does it make to know that someone is "for you" when they say hard and honest things? Do you welcome truth telling from other people? Why or why not?

2. Hannah names busyness as her "socially acceptable addiction" (p. 218). Do you believe you're important when you're busy, productive, and useful? How is God revealing the roots of this false self in you?

3. Nathan talks about the fruit of hard pruning in his life. "Our task is yielding and resting, saying yes even when God cuts off the parts we're convinced we can't live without" (p. 218). What is God pruning in you? What do you cling to as a source of significance, worth, or security? Are you able to say yes to letting go of the things that grip you?

4. What do you avoid because it is painful or uncomfortable for you?

5. **Read John 1:1-8, 19-20** slowly. Who or what is God using as a light-bringing messenger? How is the coming of light bringing life to you?

6. John the Baptist says clearly, "I am not the Messiah." In what ways have you attempted to play a messianic role for other people? Spend some time confessing these sins to God and receiving his forgiveness.

Week Eight: Day Four

∞

CHAPTER NINE: FOUND AT THE CROSSROADS
IN THE WILDERNESS (PP. 222-230)

1. **Read Psalm 121.** Then slowly read Jim Cotter's poem based on Psalm 121 (p. 222). What words or images speak to you?

2. Katherine says, "God always intends good for us. Always. There is nothing but love in God's heart for you. I promise. And because God loves you more than you can possibly comprehend, he will gently reveal areas of discomfort, pain, and agitation—not to cause you harm, but so that you can identify where it hurts and turn to him for comfort and healing" (p. 227). Do you believe that God always intends good for you? Why or why not?

3. Katherine says, "We begin our journey to freedom when we go back to the places where we were spiritually, emotionally, and mentally wounded. But this time we go with God's presence, help, and strength. No matter how frightening and messy it feels, God invites us to trust him. The Lord does some of his most beautiful work in the midst of the messiness and brokenness of our lives" (p. 227). Do you believe this? How have you experienced this to be true?

4. What is Mara afraid of? Do you share any of her fears?

5. Turn to the wilderness prayer handout (p. 224) and begin to reflect on the questions. (You will have the opportunity to ponder this handout for two days, though you may want to take longer.) As you consider the first question, you may wish to journal a timeline of your life, identifying significant events and influences that have shaped you. Or divide your life into seven-year segments and pray with the examen for those time periods. Don't rush the process. Invite God to bring to the surface what he wants you to see and name.

Week Eight: Day Five

CHAPTER NINE: FOUND AT THE CROSSROADS
IN THE WILDERNESS (PP. 222-230; SAME AS DAY FOUR)

1. Receive the words of Katherine's prayer, for yourself and for others (p. 223).

Lord . . . let your dear ones hear your voice. Let them know how tenderly you care for them, how deeply you love them. May they hear your words of healing and grace, reassuring them that you yourself have paid the price for their sin. You have purchased their freedom. Clear away any obstacles that hinder your coming into their lives. Meet them in the wilderness of their fear and shame and sorrow and regret. Come, Lord God, and make straight paths for them to travel more deeply into your heart of love. In Jesus' name. Amen.

2. Read the prayer again, making it personal. "Lord, let me hear your voice. Let me know . . ." What words or phrases catch your attention and invite your ongoing prayer?

3. Katherine pleads with the pilgrims not to walk alone (p. 229). Are you embracing God's presence offered through the companionship of fellow travelers? If not, why not?

4. Do you trust God to "bring to the surface what is ready to be healed"? (p. 230). Are you asking God to do that work in you?

5. **Read Isaiah 40:1-5.** Continue to ponder the wilderness prayer questions (p. 224) and to journal your responses and prayers.

Week Eight Group Discussion

CHAPTER EIGHT: INTIMACY AND ENCOUNTER;
CHAPTER NINE: FOUND AT THE CROSSROADS

1. Read Psalm 121 using lectio divina. What is the Holy Spirit stirring in you as you listen?

2. Discuss some moments of "intimacy and encounter" for the characters this week. Did any of their experiences or "aha" moments touch you? Why?

3. Think about your own experience of intimacy and encounter with God, others, and yourself. Are you longing for or resisting deepening intimacy? Why?

4. As you feel comfortable, share a couple of your responses to the wilderness prayer questions handout (p. 224). Where have you come from? Where are you going?

5. Name one thing you need from God right now. What can the group offer to you?

Reading for Week Nine: Chapter Nine

Week Nine: Day One

CHAPTER NINE: FOUND AT THE CROSSROADS
IN THE WILDERNESS (PP. 230-241)

1. Why does Hannah leave the group? What is she afraid of? Do you share anything in common with her?

2. What do you notice about Nathan's journey with God? Do any parts of his story resonate with you? Why or why not?

3. Are you comfortable with the image of God as Lover? Why or why not? Do you believe God's intention toward you is love?

4. In what ways is intimacy troubling for Hannah? Do you share any of those struggles?

5. Nathan says, "If I can always trust that God's intention toward me is love, then even when I don't understand the work of his hands, I can still trust his heart" (p. 241). How has this been true for you, or how might it be true for you?

6. Though the Song of Solomon was originally written as an expression of intimate love between a man and a woman, Christians have also read the text metaphorically as an intimate expression of love between God and his people. Use **Song of Solomon 2:16** as a breath prayer. As you breathe in say silently, "My beloved is mine." As you breathe out say silently, "And I am his." If, like Nathan, you struggle with the male imagery in that declaration, substitute "his" with "my beloved's."

7. Try to work this declaration of faith into the conscious rhythm of your prayers throughout the day. What does it mean for you to declare that you belong to God in love, both as lover and beloved?

Week Nine: Day Two

∽

CHAPTER NINE: FOUND AT THE CROSSROADS
PRAYING WITH IMAGINATION (PP. 242-247)

1. Katherine tells the group that she was nervous the first time she was invited to pray with her imagination: "I had such a deep respect and reverence for God's Word that I was reluctant to put any imaginary words into the text—especially into Jesus' mouth. After years of analyzing and studying biblical texts, I wasn't sure I could trust God to guide me if I started coloring outside the lines. But I began to see that the lines I'd drawn were my lines, not God's" (p. 244). Are you hesitant to read Scripture with your imagination? If so, why? What lines have you drawn around the ways you interact with God?

2. Read Meg's experience of praying with the Bartimaeus text. What catches your attention about the details she imagines? Do you connect with any of the longings she discovers?

3. **Read Mark 10:46-52.** Imagine Jesus looking intently at you and asking, "What do you want me to do for you?" How do you answer?

4. Katherine reminds the group that it's a courageous thing to ask for sight. Why? Do you want to see?

5. "Take heart; get up, he is calling you." How do you respond?

....

Week Nine: Day Three

∞

CHAPTER NINE: FOUND AT THE CROSSROADS
PRAYING WITH IMAGINATION (PP. 248-250)

1. As she imagines herself in the text, Charissa argues with Jesus about not having time to help the blind beggar. But Jesus says, "We have time, Charissa. Go and get him. Help him come to me" (p. 248). Are you bound to an agenda or schedule? Is there someone Jesus would say you really must have time for? How do you bring people into Jesus' presence?

2. Mara tells the group that she imagined herself as Bartimaeus, desperately yelling for Jesus and ignoring the people telling her to be quiet. Who is shouting, "Shut up!" or "He's not going to listen to you!" in your life? How desperately are you crying out for Jesus? Do you believe he hears you?

3. Charissa is beginning to see how deeply she has wounded others through her hardhearted judgment and condemnation. At first she wonders whether it's enough just to confess her sin privately to God. Then she realizes God wants her to humble herself and ask for Mara's forgiveness. How quick are you to humble yourself before God? Before others? Which is more difficult? Why?

4. Have you wronged anyone through your lack of love? Spend some time naming them before God and asking for forgiveness.

5. God gives Charissa both the opportunity and the courage to apologize to Mara. What words of apology would you offer the ones you have sinned against? Is there someone who could experience healing by hearing a sincere apology from you? Ask God to give you wisdom, courage, and opportunity.

6. **Read Mark 10:46-52** again. Using words or images from the story, offer your longings to God in prayer.

Week Nine: Day Four

∞

CHAPTER NINE: FOUND AT THE CROSSROADS
PRAYING WITH IMAGINATION (PP. 242-243)

1. Turn to the praying with imagination handout and enter into the story as a participant (pp. 242-243). Or, since you have already spent several days reading the text from Mark 10, you may wish to choose a different text for prayer. Select a narrative scene from one of the Gospels and use the suggestions from the handout to prayerfully enter the story. Journal what you notice as you pray.

   Alternate text suggestion: Luke 5:1-5 (deliberately stop at verse 5 to leave the story in tension).

Week Nine: Day Five

∞

CHAPTER NINE: FOUND AT THE CROSSROADS
PRAYING WITH IMAGINATION (PP. 250-254)

1. Do you freely receive and savor God's good gifts for you, or are you too busy delivering God's gifts to others?

2. Nathan identifies the flowers as symbolizing "the lover's gift to the beloved." What flowers has Jesus given you? How is Jesus inviting you to enjoy his particular affection for you?

3. Hannah sees that she left the group because of her pride—she didn't want to risk "disintegrating" in front of other people. How comfortable are you with showing frailty and weakness to others?

4. What does Hannah see in Nathan that she wants for herself? What is she willing to embrace in order to receive that gift? Are you willing to trust God in the same way?

5. What does Hannah see about God that causes her to marvel at his ways? Have you ever been surprised by God's power, grace, and providence? Spend some time remembering and recording the details.

6. **Read Song of Solomon 2:10-13.** "Arise, my darling, my beautiful one, come with me." Imagine Jesus saying these words to you. Is there anywhere you are afraid or reluctant to go with him? Why? Offer your response to God in prayer.

Week Nine Group Discussion

CHAPTER NINE: FOUND AT THE CROSSROADS

1. Using either the Bartimaeus text (Mark 10:46-52) or another Gospel narrative text, spend some time praying with imagination. What do you notice as you pray? Is this way of praying fruitful for you? Why or why not?

2. What are some "aha" moments or insights from your reflections this week?

3. How do you answer Jesus' question, "What do you want me to do for you?"

4. How confident are you in the love of God? What helps you to trust his love? What hinders your confidence in his love? How can the group pray for you?

Reading for Week Ten: Chapter Ten

Week Ten: Day One

CHAPTER TEN: DEEPER INTO THE WILDERNESS TOGETHER (PP. 255-258)

1. What evidence do you see of Hannah's movement toward God and freedom? What about Meg? Where are they still stuck?

2. Meg says to Hannah, "I'd hate for you to be so focused on what you think God's doing that you miss something else God might be doing" (p. 257). Who helps you to see how your single-minded focus can become tunnel vision? How willingly do you embrace the gift of community?

3. The image of the flowers becomes a gift for Meg as well as Hannah. Is there a word or image God has given as a gift for you to embrace and treasure—something that reminds you of his love and care for you, especially during "desolate seasons" of the soul? If not, pray about what this might be.

4. **Read 3 John 1-4** and then respond to these questions:

   - Who do you "love in the truth"? Who loves you in the truth?

   - Is your soul "getting along well"? What steps could you take toward deeper wholeness?

   - Are you faithful to the truth, walking in it with others? If not, why not?

5. What invitations do you sense from God as you read these verses? Offer your honest and heartfelt response to him.

....

Week Ten: Day Two

Chapter Ten: Deeper into the Wilderness
Hannah and Meg (pp. 258-277)

1. Hannah, like Meg, has a box of unopened grief. Meg's box holds letters from Jim. Hannah's box holds her childhood diary. What gives Hannah courage to finally open it?

2. Do you have any boxes of unspoken, unresolved issues of grief? If so, what keeps you from opening them?

3. What common patterns of communication (or lack of communication) do Meg's and Hannah's families of origin share? How did your family communicate when you were a child? How have these patterns affected you as an adult?

4. Both Hannah and Meg experienced deep wounds of abandonment as children. Was there anyone in your family who was physically, mentally, or emotionally unavailable to you? If so, how has that absence affected you?

5. "Maybe the attic revelation merely confirmed what Meg had always suspected: there was something deeper and darker to the sadness of her family. The specter of sorrow had never been named, and so it had become the air they'd breathed, poisoning them with its secrecy and silence. Now Meg had words. No reasons. No answers. But words for voicing the burden. Maybe that was gift enough" (p. 271). How is God helping you to voice your burdens and heartaches to him? To others?

6. **Read Isaiah 42:16** slowly. Then imagine God taking you by the hand and leading you into dark places. In your fear and apprehension, hear God reassure you, "I will not forsake you."

··

Week Ten: Day Three

CHAPTER TEN: DEEPER INTO THE WILDERNESS
MARA AND CHARISSA (PP. 277-281)

1. Mara has cycled around to self-pity, resentment, and despair again. What triggered this counter-movement?

2. Identify some of the triggers that lead you to move away from God into old patterns of belief and behavior. Are there any common threads that emerge? Who or what helps you to return to God?

3. News of her unexpected pregnancy reveals Charissa's ongoing struggle with self-absorption and a desire for control. With whom are you more sympathetic: Charissa or John? Why?

4. As John nurses his own disappointment and heartache, he second-guesses whether Charissa has experienced any authentic transformation. "John had witnessed so much evidence of spiritual and emotional growth in her the past few weeks, and now it seemed to have completely evaporated. In an instant—gone" (p. 281). How do you view setbacks in your own spiritual growth or in the growth of those who are close to you? Are you patient with the process of transformation in yourself? In others?

5. What do you do with deep disappointments? Are you able to speak honestly about them with others and with God, or do you bury them?

6. **Read Philippians 1:6** out loud several times. What good work has God begun in you? How is God carrying that work forward, even when it's

difficult to see any fruit of transformation? Spend some time thanking God that his work is not fragile or temporary. Find a way to celebrate his faithfulness today.

Week Ten: Day Four

CHAPTER TEN: DEEPER INTO THE WILDERNESS
MEG (PP. 281-284)

1. Katherine offers Meg an image of a pearl being formed, sometimes by a grain of sand, other times by a parasitic intruder. "At first the oyster tries to get rid of it. But if it can't, it encloses the intruder into a sac. Then the oyster begins coating the sac with mother of pearl—the same substance that lines the shell. The oyster adds layer after layer for the rest of its life" (p. 282). How does this image speak to you about the process of healing and transformation?

2. Katherine says, "Life's painful intrusions aren't negotiable, are they? They happen. It's what we do with them that matters" (p. 282). Katherine then names some of the unhealthy ways she's seen people respond

to pain. How have you responded to life's painful intrusions? Is this the way Jesus offers?

3. How have you experienced Jesus as the redeemer of your sorrow and suffering? Do you see any evidence that he is creating something beautiful out of your pain?

4. Katherine once invited Meg to stop trying to get over her fears and instead offer them to God. Now she counsels her in a similar way regarding grief. "God never says, 'Just get over it,' Meg. Never. God says, 'Give it to me.' And there's an enormous difference between the two" (p. 284). What's the difference? In which way have you dealt with grief? Why?

5. Katherine says, "It's easier to stay in denial. We can hear voices in our heads, saying, 'Remember how painful it was the first time? You certainly don't want to go back and go through it all again!' But the path to freedom and healing takes us right through the heart of the pain. Jesus the Good Shepherd walks with you through the darkness.... You're not alone. Never alone" (p. 284). Have you asked God for the courage to grieve well? Are you confident of his presence with you as you walk through the heart of pain?

6. **Read Isaiah 43:1-2** slowly, inserting your name and receiving God's promises.

....

Week Ten: Day Five

CHAPTER TEN: DEEPER INTO THE WILDERNESS
MARA AND TOGETHER (PP. 285-287)

1. As she sits in her counselor's office, Mara notices a two-dimensional figure of a little girl with her arms raised high above her head, her outstretched hands open wide in a posture of trust and joy. Dawn asks, "Is she receiving or letting go?" Mara observes that it's impossible to tell—it's the same gesture for both (p. 285). What does this image mean to you? Do you live with your hands open?

2. Mara says it was easier to forgive Charissa because she said she was sorry. How do you forgive people who never apologize?

3. The experience of forgiving Charissa has triggered pain from old wounds, things Mara has tried hard to forget. Have you ever had a similar experience? What does Mara see about God's work in the midst of her struggle?

4. What kind of letters is Mara writing? Why is she writing them? Are there any letters for you to write?

5. **Read Isaiah 51:12-16.** Who or what is oppressing you? How is God "stirring up the sea" to get your attention? What is the pathway to freedom that God has provided for you? Using words or images from the text, offer your prayer to God.

Week Ten Group Discussion

Chapter Ten: Deeper into the Wilderness

1. Read 3 John 1-4 using lectio divina. What is the Holy Spirit revealing to you as you listen?

2. Which characters do you find yourself resonating with this week? Frustrated by? Why?

3. Given what the characters are experiencing, what kinds of windows or mirrors are opening into your own life with God right now? How do you feel about what you see?

4. What next steps do you sense God inviting you to take as you travel "deeper into the wilderness"? How can the group pray for you?

Reading for Week Eleven: Chapter Eleven

Week Eleven: Day One

CHAPTER ELEVEN: LIGHTENING THE LOAD
CONFESSION (PP. 288-296)

1. How does Charissa feel about the topic of confession? Do you share anything in common with her?

2. Katherine describes freedom as "being able to say, 'Yes, that's my sin. And yes, I have a Savior.' No need to hide. No need to be defensive. No need to be ashamed. No need to carry the burden of trying to be perfect. We have freedom to confess what's true about ourselves and receive God's grace" (p. 289). Have you experienced this kind of freedom? Do you earnestly desire this kind of freedom? What steps could you take in order to walk in deeper freedom and the joy of grace?

3. How do you respond when someone criticizes you? Do you listen to discern whether there's any truth in the criticism, or do you quickly respond by being defensive, bitter, or angry? Do you try to collect allies who affirm your right to be upset?

4. What's the difference between "self-examination" and "self-scrutiny for the sake of perfecting ourselves"?

5. How does John hold grace, truth, and love together in his conversation with Charissa? Do you believe there is ever "too much grace"? Have you ever poured out extravagant grace to someone else? Received it from someone else? Spend some time remembering what those experiences were like for you.

6. Meditate on **2 Corinthians 7:8-10**. What is the difference between worldly sorrow and godly sorrow? Is the revelation of your sin leading you to Jesus and to life, or to regret and death? Offer your prayer to God.

Week Eleven: Day Two

∽

CHAPTER ELEVEN: LIGHTENING THE LOAD
CONFESSION (PP. 291-292)

1. **Read Psalm 51:6-13.** Then turn to the self-examination and confession handout and prayerfully journal your responses.

Week Eleven: Day Three

∽

CHAPTER ELEVEN: LIGHTENING THE LOAD
(MULTIPLE SECTIONS, PP. 296-308)

1. Mara's letter writing has given Meg an idea for how she can move forward in her grieving process. Have you ever written letters like the ones Meg writes to Jim or to her father? Is there a "goodbye" or "I forgive you" letter you need to write?

2. Hannah writes, "Maybe part of my progress is realizing what triggers me and catching it more quickly each time. Help, Lord. Help. I can't change myself. I spiral so quickly into regret. Please help me fix my eyes on you. Please" (p. 299). What does progress look like for you?

3. Hannah tells Meg, "We can only let go of the things we first hold on to" (p. 305). What do you think she means by that?

4. Mara and Charissa each experience significant pain within their families. If you were their friend, what would you counsel them to do? What do you do when the people close to you hurt or disappoint you?

5. **Read Isaiah 9:2, 4.** Using words or images from the text, offer your longings to God in prayer.

Week Eleven: Day Four

CHAPTER ELEVEN: LIGHTENING THE LOAD
HANNAH (pp. 308-318)

1. What do you notice about Nathan's interaction with Hannah at lunch? Do you have friends who consistently ask where you are with God? Are you honest with them?

2. Meg says to Hannah, "I remember you told me once how kind the Spirit is to reveal what we need to know, when we need to know it. And I don't want to resist what God's doing. I want to stay attentive" (p. 312). Have you experienced the kindness and gentleness of the Spirit revealing what you need to know, when you need to know it? Do you want to stay attentive, or do you find yourself wrestling and resisting, like Hannah?

3. Meg has hung a picture of Jesus tenderly embracing a little lamb with his nail-scarred hand on the door to her parents' bedroom as a reminder of being held in her grief and fear. (The sketch is *Jesus and the Lamb* by Katherine Brown, and you can view it online.) On what closed doors in your life do you need to place a reminder of Jesus' love and care? What words, promises, or images do you need to put there? Write down some

verses that strengthen and encourage you, or describe an image that brings you peace.

4. Why does Hannah finally speak her truth out loud? Are there people you have been able to tell the whole truth to? If not, seek God about who you could confide in.

5. Hannah immediately tries to figure out what she is supposed to do next. But Meg says, "It's all one step at a time, remember? You don't need to have it all figured out. Maybe it's enough to lay the burden down. You've been carrying so much for so long. Just rest, Hannah. Rest" (p. 318). Is there any word of truth for you in this? Is resting "hard work" for you? Why?

6. **Read Matthew 11:28-30.** Using the palms-up, palms-down prayer, spend some time handing your burdens over to Jesus. What does he give you in exchange?

Week Eleven: Day Five

Chapter Eleven: Lightening the Load

1. Take some time simply to rest. Do something special that brings you life. Look ahead on your schedule over the next few months. Consider putting an X through one day each week as a sabbath day.

Week Eleven Group Discussion

CHAPTER ELEVEN: LIGHTENING THE LOAD

1. Turn to page 291 in the book, read Genesis 3:1-9 together, and then discuss your responses to the handout questions. Is there anything you feel led to confess in the safety of this group?

2. If there's time remaining, discuss any other insights or movement forward this week. How can you encourage one another to persevere in hope?

Reading for Week Twelve:
Chapter Twelve and Epilogue

....

Week Twelve: Days One and Two

∞

CHAPTER TWELVE: WALKING TOGETHER IN THE LOVE OF GOD
RULE OF LIFE (PP. 319-327)

1. Review some of the practices mentioned in the book. There are many others to consider as you move forward in your life with God. (Two good resources are *Celebration of Discipline* by Richard Foster and *Spiritual Disciplines Handbook* by Adele Ahlberg Calhoun.)

2. **Read John 15:9** several times slowly. Then turn to the rule of life handout (pp. 321-322) and begin to identify the practices that help you receive, remain in, and respond to the love of God. Remember to consider both individual and corporate practices, practices that are life giving and ones that stretch you beyond what is comfortable, and practices that help you receive God's love and offer that love to others.

Week Twelve: Day Three

CHAPTER TWELVE: WALKING TOGETHER IN THE LOVE OF GOD
REVELATION (PP. 327-336)

1. As Hannah walks the labyrinth alone, she ponders how she is traveling deeper into the heart of God. Where does she need to fix her attention, especially when the path seems circuitous and disorienting? Where are you fixing your attention?

2. Hannah experiences a holy moment when she sees and really embraces that she has the full, loving, and undivided attention of the God who flung galaxies into space. Have you had a holy moment when you realized and embraced God's unconditional, lavish love for you? What or who does God use to reveal his love for you?

3. When Hannah shares her newfound joy with Nathan, he says, "You spent the first part [of your sabbatical] unpacking some of your grief points and sitting with some of the sorrow. Maybe the next part is about entering into rest and joy and really basking in God's particular love for you—

whatever that looks like in your life" (p. 330). How can you practice celebration? What does relaxing into God look like for you?

4. Hannah finally sees the root reasons for her self-denial and over-developed sense of responsibility. Is there any experience from your past that still needs to be named as a source of captivity for you? Who helps you hear the tragedy in your own story in order to help you receive God's healing power?

5. Hannah realizes that her childhood coping mechanisms served their purpose for a season, helping her hold her life together. But now those coping mechanisms are hindrances and obstacles to her freedom. Have you developed any similar ways of coping that God is inviting you to lay down? How is God inviting you to trust him?

6. Slowly and prayerfully read **Ephesians 3:16-19**. Receive Paul's prayer for yourself and begin to pray it for others.

Week Twelve: Day Four

EPILOGUE

1. What remains unresolved for each of the women? What next steps do you hope they take?

2. What are you celebrating about your journey thus far? What next steps do you hope to take? Who will walk with you as you continue the sacred journey?

3. **Read Psalm 91:1-4.** What promises will you carry forward as you continue your sacred journey?

Week Twelve: Day Five

1. Spend some time reviewing your twelve-week pilgrimage. What testimony would you add to the New Hope website? (p. 50).

2. Return to any unfinished questions you marked along the way. Is there anything else you're ready to answer now?

3. Use **Ephesians 3:20-21** as a way of thanking God for all he has already done and for all he has yet to do.

   God is faithful. So faithful. And there's so much joy in the journey! My prayer for each of you is that you grow in trust. May you grow in the knowledge of God's deep love for you. May you learn to relax into God and rest in his power and faithfulness. May you find opportunities to love God and love others. And since God made us for life together, may you find trustworthy companions to walk with you along the way. (p. 326)

Week Twelve Group Discussion

Chapter Twelve: Walking Together in the Love of God; Epilogue

1. Read Ephesians 3:16-19 using lectio divina. What are you noticing as you listen to the text?

2. Share with one another from your rules of life. Are you open to receiving feedback and input from the group about what to consider including (like the characters offered to one another)? If so, prayerfully offer those insights to each other.

3. Spend some time encouraging one another. Take turns so that each person hears affirmation. What have you noticed about each other's progress as you've walked together? What are you celebrating?

4. What next steps do you hope the characters take? What next steps do you hope to take, individually and as a group?

5. Turn back to week two, day one, question two. What did you hope twelve weeks ago that you would be saying at the end of the study? What testimony would you write now for the New Hope Center website?

6. Read Ephesians 3:20-21 in unison as a way of thanking God for what he has done and for what he will do.

Now to him who is able to do immeasurably more than all we ask or imagine, according to his power that is at work within us, to him be glory in the church and in Christ Jesus throughout all generations, for ever and ever! Amen.

The Sensible Shoes Series

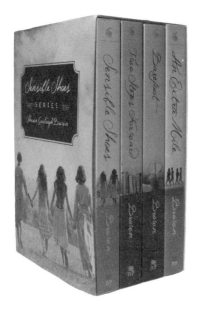

Sensible Shoes

Two Steps Forward

Barefoot

An Extra Mile

STUDY GUIDES

For more information about the Sensible Shoes series,
visit ivpress.com/sensibleshoesseries.
To learn more from Sharon Garlough Brown or to sign up for her newsletter,
go to ivpress.com/sharon-news.